THE ADVENTURES OF PUSS IN BOOTS, JR.

Nadakkavu, Kozhikode, Kerala, 673011
www.insightpublica.com
e-mail: insightpublica@gmail.com
Title: **THE ADVENTURES OF PUSS IN BOOTS, JR**
Author: **DAVID CORY**
First Insight Edition: May 2025
Printed and Published by
InsightinPublica Printers & Publishers Pvt. Ltd.
ISBN: 978-93-5517-825-1
₹ 170

THE ADVENTURES OF PUSS IN BOOTS, JR.

DAVID CORY

CONTENTS

PUSS IN BOOTS, JR., BEGINS HIS TRAVELS

PUSS had made a great discovery in the garret. It seems strange that he should have found something more important than a rat or mouse, but he had. From the moment he had seen the picture-book he was a changed cat!

"Yes," he said, holding it a little to one side, so that the light from the small attic window would show the picture more distinctly, "this is certainly a portrait of my father."

It was the story of "Puss in Boots," and on the cover was a beautiful picture of a cat wearing a magnificent pair of boots with shiny red tops. Puss sat down and opened the book. The further he read the more excited he became. When he had finished he jumped up and, proudly looking at the portrait of his handsome father, he exclaimed, with flashing eyes, "From to-day I shall call myself 'Puss in Boots, Junior'; I shall go forth in search of adventure, just as my father did, and I shall not rest until I have found him!"

He looked around to see if he could find a pair of boots like those in the picture.

To his delight he saw in a corner the very pair he wanted, and they had red tops, too. He slipped them on and looked at himself in an old cracked mirror which stood against the wall.

On a peg near by hung a cap, dusty, but not a bit shabby or worn. Placing it on his head, he hunted around until he found an old cane with a bent handle. "There's a cane in the picture—I suppose they called it a staff in those days; at any rate, I'm now complete; I'm a real Puss in Boots, Junior!" and with these words he scampered down the stairs as fast as he dared, not yet being used to his new-found boots.

"Hurray!" he cried, as he reached the front door, and he took a hop, skip, and jump across the piazza, holding his tail gracefully in his left paw. "Hurray!"

Down the steps he skipped, two at a time, down the walk to the gate, his heels clattering on the stone pavement, rat-a-tat-tat, like a cavalryman. The road was dusty, but he went along gaily, the sun shining on the bright-red tops of his boots, making him very proud indeed.

He hadn't gone very far when he heard a funny little squeak, and, looking to the side of the road from which the sound came, he saw a small pig stuck between two boards in the fence.

"Squeak, squeak! Oh, help me out!" cried Piggie.

Puss in Boots, Jr., ran up and, with the help of his cane, pried the boards apart so that the little pig could just squeeze himself through. "Squeak, squeak! Oh, thank you!" cried the little fellow. "I wish I could do something to repay you!"

"You can," replied Puss, Jr., who had by this time grown very hungry, "I would like something to eat."

"Come with me," said Piggie. "Mother always gets some milk from the dairymaid about this time. Come." And he took Puss, Jr., by the front paw and started to run across the field.

"Hold on! I mean, let go!" cried Puss in Boots, Jr. "How do you know your mother will want visitors for lunch?"

"She'll be only too delighted, especially when she knows how you pulled me out of the fence. You're not bashful, are you?"

"No-o-o!" replied Puss, Jr., "but you see I've never lunched with pigs before!"

"Oh, don't let that worry you," replied his little friend, who seemed to be pretty sure of himself for so small a pig. "Come along!"

And Puss did.

A VISIT TO PIGGIE'S MAMMA

PUSS, JR., followed his friend the little pig, whom he had so fortunately rescued from between the fence boards, across the field and into the woods. Indeed, he was so hungry by this time that he felt he would be brave enough to follow a lion. Just then he heard some one singing in a high, squeaky voice:

"This little Pig went to market,

This little Pig stayed at home,

This little Pig had roast beef,

This little Pig had none,

This little Pig cried, 'Wee, wee, wee!'

All the way home."

"That's mother," replied the little pig in answer to an inquiring look from Puss, Jr. "She always sings that when any of us is naughty. You see," he added, apologetically, "I should not have tried to get through the fence and out on the road."

"Oh, I understand," replied Puss, Jr. "Is that your house?"

"Yes, and there's mother."

Puss, Jr., saw a very nice-looking lady pig standing in

the doorway of a queer little cabin. She had on a blue gingham apron over a short skirt of gray, and a very tight-fitting shirt-waist, which was stretched almost to the bursting-point as she raised her right forefoot to shade her eyes.

"Well, here you are at last!" she exclaimed to Piggie. "But look at your trousers; you've torn a big hole in them!"

He looked ruefully at the rent in his little blue jeans. "I got stuck in the fence," he whimpered.

"He'd be there yet if I hadn't pulled him out," volunteered Puss, Jr., hoping to divert her attention from his little friend.

Mrs. Porker, for that was her name, turned and looked at him, as much as to say, "Where did you come from?" but she didn't; she only very politely remarked: "Thank you for helping Piggie. I'm sorry to say he does not always mind mother. But come, you both are hungry, I know." And she led the way into the cabin.

At a round table in the room two little pigs were already eating their dinner. "What is your name?" asked Mrs. Porker in a kindly tone, pushing a chair up next to hers for Puss.

"Puss in Boots, Junior, madam," he replied, with a polite bow.

"This is Wiggie and this is Tiggie," said their mother, and the two small pigs got up and shook hands with him.

They had a merry lunch, and he was surprised to see how clean and well behaved the Porker family was.

"You know," said Mrs. Porker, as if reading his thoughts, "that pigs are really the cleanest of animals, only man is so cruel to pigs—he shuts them up in small pens and makes them appear quite the opposite. Just read the books about us and you will see. Yes," she continued, "when pigs are allowed to run around they are clean as they can be; only when they are little they are often most disobedient." And she looked at Piggie, who got very red in the face.

"I don't believe he'll disobey again," answered Puss, Jr. "You have such a nice playground here in the woods I shouldn't think he would want to run away to that dusty road again; just look at my boots." And he thrust his foot out and showed the bright-red tops all dingy with the day's travel.

Lunch was now over, and after politely thanking Mrs. Porker for her goodness Puss said good-by to the three little pigs.

"Don't forget me," called out Piggie as Puss, Jr., climbed over the fence.

"Of course I won't," he called back, and waved his paw to Piggie in the doorway.

PUSS SEES THE COW JUMP OVER THE MOON

PUSS, JR., trudged along bravely for some time, but, finding it very dusty, he left the road and climbed over the low stone wall that bordered the big pasture on his right.

"It's funny to see the moon in the daytime," he remarked as he crossed the long green meadow dotted everywhere with yellow cowslips; "I don't understand it," and he looked curiously at the big, white moon which hung low in the skies just overhead. As he spoke, across the grass hopped a big silver spoon, closely followed by a dish with a blue border, which rolled along over the ground at a great rate.

"Wow, wow! Ha, ha!" laughed a little dog from the other side of the fence. "Keep on rolling; you'll tire him out pretty soon."

Puss, Jr., watched the funny race with much amusement until he was startled by a voice at his side, saying, "Glad to see you," and, turning around, he saw a small cat with a fiddle under her paw.

"Hey diddle-diddle," she sang in a high, sweet voice, and scratched away on the strings like a player in an orchestra.

PUSS, JR., TRUDGED ALONG BRAVELY

"Tell me," Puss, Jr., said to her as the music stopped for a moment, "why is the moon out to-day? I thought it only came out at night."

"Why, don't you know?" she replied. "It is going to let the cow jump over it to-day."

"Indeed! and when does that happen?"

"Oh, any minute now; in fact, there she comes through the gate." And, sure enough, across the fields a beautiful black-and-white cow came leisurely toward them.

"Good morning," she exclaimed, as she neared our two friends, and, turning to the cat with the fiddle, she said: "Are you ready? If you are, just strike up a lively tune so that I can get into step before I try for my jump."

Puss, Jr., was so interested that he forgot to ask another question, but stood still while the cow commenced to prance around, keeping perfect time to the music.

"Faster, faster!" she called, as she swung into a canter. "I'm going to get a flying start; you know, if you get a flying start the higher you will fly when you do fly."

This undoubtedly was true, for in a moment more she rose gracefully from the ground toward the moon.

"Be careful!" screamed the Man in the Moon, leaning out as she approached near enough for his voice to reach her. "Be careful and don't clip off a piece with your hoof as you go over!"

She did as he told her, and sailed over in a long, sweeping curve and landed safely in a patch of clover at the other end of the field.

"Great!" exclaimed Puss, Jr. "You did it splendidly!"

"Oh, that's nothing!" she answered, although she seemed rather proud of her feat. "Oh, that's nothing at all!"

"I don't agree with you," he replied. "I should think you'd be very proud of your feet; they're as good as wings."

The Jumping Cow paid no more attention to him, but munched away at the clover like an ordinary cow.

"She won't say another word to-day," whispered the cat behind her fiddle; "but if you're around this way to-morrow morning and it's a nice day she may try another jump."

"I'm sorry," Puss, Jr., replied, "but by that time I shall be far away upon my journey. Thank you just the same." And with these words he took off his hat to Miss Pussy and resumed his travels along the cool, shady path through the woods.

PUSS MEETS YANKEE DOODLE DANDY

THE broad highway was somewhat dusty and not nearly so pleasant as the cool, shady path through the woods. At the same time Puss felt that it was leading him on toward his journey's end, and the thought that then he would find his dear father made his heart beat fast with hope.

He began to whistle, when suddenly he heard the sound of hoofbeats. Then a voice commenced singing, loudly and clearly:

"Yankee Doodle came to town,

Riding on a pony;

He stuck a feather in his cap

And called it macaroni.

"Yankee Doodle came to town,

Yankee Doodle dandy,

He stuck a feather in his cap

And called it sugar candy."

Down the road came a pony at a mad gallop, and seated upon his back was a very queer-looking person. In his cap was a long feather and in his right hand was a big whip. The pony was galloping along at a great rate, and every now and again his rider would give a tremendous whoop, like an Indian brave. "Yankee Doodle Dandy!" he yelled, and then the pony would stand up on his hind legs and neigh.

"Look out!" yelled the rider, as he approached Puss. "Don't you see you are in the way?"

"Am I?" said Puss, drawing to one side of the road.

"Well, not now," said the rider, drawing rein and looking at Puss with a good deal of interest. "Where's your horse?"

"Where's my horse?" repeated Puss, looking about as if he expected to find one.

"Yes, where's your steed?" continued the stranger.

"Haven't got any," said Puss. "My two legs are all that I have to carry me."

"Get up behind me," said the stranger. "My name is Yankee Doodle Dandy, and a Yankee is always willing to give a fellow-traveler a lift, whether he be on the high seas or on the road."

"Thank you, my fellow-traveler," replied Puss, and he sprang nimbly to the saddle and clung tightly to the coat-tails of Yankee Doodle Dandy.

"Git-ap!" cried the latter, and away went the pony down the road. In a short time the towers and church steeples of a town came into view.

Suddenly a queer-looking figure tumbled down from the sky on to the road just in front of them. Yankee Doodle Dandy reined in his horse just in time; otherwise he would have run over the Man in the Moon.

"Why don't you fall any other place but right in front of my horse?" asked Yankee Doodle Dandy, in a stern voice.

"Couldn't help it," answered the Man in the Moon. "You must remember it's not such an easy thing to hit the exact spot you intend to when you jump all the way from the moon. It's almost impossible. I've even heard that an aeroplane has some difficulty in dropping bombs so that they hit the mark."

"Well, I've heard that, too," admitted Yankee Doodle Dandy, "although up to this time Yankeeville has not suffered from any air attacks."

"Well, don't be too sure," answered the Man in the Moon. "I've seen a few things from my moon house that you never even dreamed of."

"Did you never hear the rhyme about the Man in the Moon?" Puss asked, politely.

"No, I never did," said the Man in the Moon.

"What!" exclaimed Puss in surprise.

"The Man in the Moon came tumbling down

And asked the way to Norwich;

He went by the south and burnt his mouth

With eating cold pease porridge."

"Ha, ha!" laughed the Man in the Moon, "you are joking; I'm sure you are," and he turned his footsteps toward the south.

"'He went by the south and burnt his mouth,'" said Puss.

"We can't help it," said Yankee Doodle; "he will go that way."

PUSS SINGS A SONG AND HELPS A BEGGAR

AFTER he had said good-by to Yankee Doodle Dandy, Puss, Jr., had a good time playing all the morning with some little boys whom he met. One of the little boys got out his hobby-horse and he and Puss, Jr., took turns galloping up and down the sidewalk.

"I had a little hobby-horse,

And it was dapple gray;

Its head was made of pea straw,

Its tail was made of hay,"

sang his mother from the front porch. "My little boy has had a fine time," she said, "but he must come in now and rest, for it is almost luncheon-time."

"And I must be going," said Puss, Jr., "for I have many miles yet to travel ere I find my father, Puss in Boots."

"You have been so kind," said the little boy's mother as she shook hands with Puss.

"Good-by!" cried the little boy, quite sorrowfully, waving his hat as Puss disappeared down the street.

"Heigh-ho!" said Puss to himself, "once more on my

journey. I'm a wandering minstrel, as it were," and to suit
his words he began to sing:

"A wandering little cat am I,

Seeking father cat,

In my paw my trusty staff,

On my head my hat

With the magic plume the owl

Gave to me one day.

When the journey ends I'll have

Lots of time to play!"

"A pussy-cat poet!" cried a voice close at hand.

Puss, Jr., started and turned. At his side stood a beggar-man.

"I'm hungry," said the poor fellow, "and poets, I hear, are
always generous," and he held out his hat for Puss to drop
in a penny.

"Are they?" inquired Puss, with a grin; he put his hand
into his pocket and took out a sixpence. "Here, my good
man," he said, "take this little piece of money. It is more
than I will get for the song which you seem to admire so
much.

"What are you going to buy with the money?" he asked,
after they had walked along for some time. They had left
the city and were now in the country.

"I'm going to get some pease porridge hot," answered
the beggar. "I'm going to spend that sixpence in short order!
I haven't had a thing to eat since yesterday morning."

"I have never gone hungry so long as that," said Puss. "I
think I've been pretty lucky since I started out to find my
father, Puss in Boots."

"Puss in Boots!" exclaimed the beggar-man with sur-

"WHAT ARE YOU GOING TO BUY WITH THE MONEY?" PUSS ASKED

prise. "Why, I once stopped at a castle where there was a most wonderful cat. He was the seneschal, I think, and a most intelligent animal."

"Where was the castle?" asked Puss. "I mean, in what country?"

"I don't remember," replied the beggar-man. "You see, I have begged at so many back doors and so many postern gates that I have them all jumbled up together in my memory."

"Dear me," said Puss. "Will I ever find anybody who really knows where my father lives?"

"Pease porridge hot,

Pease porridge cold,

Pease porridge in the pot,

Nine days old."

Along the road came a man with a big white apron over his coat. In front of him he wheeled a little cart in which was a large pot of porridge.

"Some like it hot,

Some like it cold,

Some like it in the pot,

Nine days old."

"Well, it won't be in that pot even nine minutes!" cried the beggar-man. "Here, my good friend," he cried, "give me sixpence worth of your porridge, and be quick about it."

"Don't be in a hurry," said the porridge-man. "Where's the sixpence?"

"Here in my good right hand," replied the beggar-man.

"Ah!" said the porridge-man, "you shall have your porridge."

"I will also have some," said Puss.

"Hot or cold?" asked the man.

"You take yours hot and I'll take mine cold," said the beggar-man, and in a few minutes the porridge was all gone.

PUSS FOLLOWS WEE WILLIE WINKIE

THE vesper bells were ringing as Puss, Jr., entered the great gate that led into the city of Babylon. Along the street the lamps were being lighted and their flickering gleams sent the shadows hiding in building and alley.

Puss, however, in spite of shadows, trudged on with a brave heart, waiting for an opportunity to get his supper and a comfortable place to sleep.

Suddenly he was startled by a strange sight. A small boy in his nightgown came racing down the street:

"Wee Willie Winkie runs through the town,

Up-stairs and down-stairs in his nightgown,

Rapping at the windows, crying through the lock,

'Are the children in their beds? It's past eight o'clock!'"

"Wait for me!" cried Puss, Jr., but Wee Willie Winkie did not stop. On he ran, turning the next corner before Puss could overtake him. Half-way down the block Puss stopped and ran up the steps of a small house. Lifting the big brass knocker, he let it fall with a rap that soon brought a maid to the door.

"Goodness me!" she exclaimed. "What have we here?"

"Is anybody at home?" said Puss, flicking the dust off the red tops of his boots in a most unconcerned way, as if, indeed, he had been accustomed to making calls all his life.

The maid held out a little silver tray. "I will take your card."

Poor Puss! He didn't have any!

"But I'm Puss in Boots, Junior," he said, with such a lovely purr that the maid opened the door wide:

"Come in, dear Puss, Junior."

Just then Wee Willie Winkie ran down the stairs, crying: "Are the children in their beds? It's past eight o'clock." Closing the front door, he whispered through the keyhole, "Are the children in their beds?" And before he reached the sidewalk he turned back and, rapping on the window, cried, "It's past eight o'clock!"

"Little kittens don't need Wee Willie Winkie, I guess," said the maid, tickling Puss, Jr.'s, head.

"Hush-a-bye, baby, lie still with thy daddy;

Thy mammy has gone to the mill

To get some meal to bake a cake,

So pray, my dear baby, lie still."

The lullaby made Puss, Jr., sleepy, for the man's voice was low and tender, and Puss was very tired.

In a sleepy voice he asked, "And has the mother gone to the mill to get the meal for the cake?"

"Indeed she has," replied the maid.

After this she went into the kitchen. Puss gazed about him for a while and then dropped off to sleep, hearing the drowsy voice of the man up-stairs singing:

"Hush-a-bye, baby, lie still with thy daddy."

All was very quiet. "Tick-tock, tick-tock," said the big

clock, and a mouse peeped out of his hole and laughed to himself when he saw Puss fast asleep. He tiptoed over to the red-topped boots that had fallen off Puss, Jr.'s, tired little feet, and even crawled inside. Perhaps he wanted to tell his father how brave he had been to go inside a big cat's high-top boots while the owner snored close by. Presently he ran over to the hole in the wall. I imagine it did not take him long to tell his story, for in a few minutes three little mice crept out and tiptoed over to where Puss lay sleeping so soundly.

"Did you ever see any nicer boots than these?"

Mr. Mouse put on a very wise expression.

"They are certainly a very fine pair of boots," said he, "and they have the mark of a royal cobbler."

"Gracious me! how interesting!" cried Mrs. Mouse; "let me take a look." And she inspected Puss, Jr.'s, footwear with much interest. "Beautifully made," she said. "This must be a royal cat, for otherwise why should he have a royal cobbler?"

"I only hope he is not a royal mouser," replied Mr. Mouse, "and I think, now that we have seen all we have, we had better return, for who knows when he may awake?"

So they scampered off, leaving Puss, Jr., still sound asleep.

PUSS, JR., MEETS THREE JOLLY WELSHMEN AND THE QUEEN OF HEARTS

AS Puss, Jr., staff in hand, wandered down the green hills to the lowlands, he came to a sandy beach, and there stood three jolly Welshmen looking toward the sea:

One said it was a ship,

The other he said "Nay,"

The third one said it was a house

With the chimney blown away.

"It's nothing of the sort," cried Puss, Jr., jumping nimbly about, "it's nothing of the sort."

"Perhaps it's a submarine," suggested one of the three jolly Welshmen, walking over to inspect the little craft.

"Wrong again," tooted a little owl who was perched upon a tree close by.

"It looks like a cheese," suggested the smallest of the three jolly Welshmen.

"Nonsense," answered Puss, Jr. "Who ever heard of a person sailing about in a cheese?"

"Well, I didn't mean a Swiss cheese," replied the Welshman who up to this time had said nothing. "Swiss cheeses are full of holes. I guess they wouldn't float very long."

"This boat has a big crack in it," said Puss. "Just look and see for yourself."

"Crackers and cheese!" laughed one of the three jolly Welshmen. "How do you like my joke?"

"It makes me feel hungry," said Puss, Jr. "I've had nothing to eat for a long time."

"Come with us, then," said the three jolly Welshmen; "we'll take you to see the Queen."

PUSS JOINED IN THE CHASE TO HELP THE QUEEN

"I don't look very neat," replied Puss, rubbing the salt spray from his boot-tops.

"Neither do I," cried the little owl, preening his feathers and stretching out his tail. "I'm all ruffled up."

"Well, the Queen's making tarts to-day," cried the three jolly Welshmen all at once. "We're going, anyway."

Puss, Jr., and the little owl waited no longer, but followed the three Welshmen at once. In the distance could be seen the turrets of a stately castle. On arriving at the postern gate they were admitted after a slight delay. In the courtyard all was bustle and excitement. On long tables were spread the most delicious-looking tarts—raspberry, strawberry, lemon, apple, and all the other delicious varieties that could be imagined. Puss, Jr.'s, mouth fairly watered at the sight, and the little owl could hardly restrain himself from picking out strawberries that protruded from under the crust of a tart near at hand. The three jolly Welshmen also showed signs of impatience. They were as anxious to taste the tarts as were their small companions.

At that instant a great commotion arose. The Knave of Hearts was seen rushing away with a whole trayful of tarts. After him ran the Queen, holding up her long train so as to run faster. Puss joined in the chase to help the Queen.

PUSS LEARNS WHERE HIS FATHER IS AND RECEIVES A TART FROM THE QUEEN

THE Knave of Hearts was a pretty good runner, and Puss, Jr., found it no easy task to catch him. Finally, however, he did, and after some difficulty brought him back to the castle. As they entered the postern gate,

The King of Hearts

Called for those tarts,

And beat the Knave full sore.

"I'm glad I didn't take a tart," said Puss, in a whisper to his little friend the owl, while the three jolly Welshmen looked much relieved to think that they had not touched one, either. At this point the Queen came graciously forward and offered them all a tart apiece.

"How do you like it?" she asked Puss, smiling in a kind way. "You deserve much more than a tart for having caught that naughty Knave. What can I do to reward you?"

Puss carefully wiped his whiskers with his pocket-handkerchief before replying. "Your Majesty," he answered, "I am in search of my illustrious father, Puss in Boots. Could you but direct me to him I shall consider you have more than repaid me for my trouble."

"Come into the castle," said the Queen, "and I will have my seneschal inquire. No doubt he will know, as he is a very wise man and an old retainer." So saying, she led the way into the castle, followed by Puss, Jr., and the little owl.

"Puss in Boots? Puss in Boots?" repeated the old man, in an inquiring tone, talking half to himself. "Why, is he not in the employ of my Lord of Carabas?"

"Yes, indeed!" cried the Queen. "Now I remember. My dear Puss in Boots, Junior, you still have a long journey before you; but to the brave all things are possible. Although he lives far beyond the border-line of Mother Goose Land, a good traveler need not despair."

"No, indeed, your Highness," replied Puss, Jr., "I have a good heart and strong legs. 'Tis but a question of time before I see him, for danger I fear not, neither stony roads nor stormy seas."

"Bravely said," cried the Queen. "But who is your little friend?" she added, turning to look at the owl, who had perched himself on the shoulder of Puss, Jr.

"He is the owner of the 'beautiful pea-green boat,'" replied Puss, "and to him I owe much, for had he not come to my rescue when the Giant of the Bean-stalk pursued me I should have been captured. His boat was on the shore and we sailed away just in time."

"Most exciting," said the Queen; "and so that is how you landed on Cranberry Tart Island?"

"Yes, your Highness," said Puss, "but I did not know it was an island nor that it was called 'Cranberry Tart.'"

"Well, it is," replied the Queen, "and if you will spend the night here I will see that you reach the mainland to-morrow without delay."

So Puss, Jr., consented to spend the night in the stately castle of Tart Island.

PUSS CROSSES A WONDERFUL BRIDGE

THE next morning, bright and early, Puss, Jr., left the stately castle of Cranberry Tart Island and continued his journey. The Queen had bidden him a kind farewell, at the same time instructing one of her retainers to show him the bridge connecting Cranberry Tart Island with the mainland.

On arriving at the bridge Puss, Jr., was most surprised to see that it was built entirely of gingerbread. "Goodness!" he exclaimed to himself, "if many stopped on their way over to take a bite, there would soon be no bridge left."

Probably the builder had been aware of this fact, for at the entrance of the bridge was displayed a large sign which read as follows:

No loitering allowed on the bridge. The gingerbread must not be eaten, under penalty of a fine and imprisonment.

"It looks pretty stale, anyway," tooted the little owl, who blinked and winked in the early morning light as he flew beside Puss, Jr.

"You can't see very well, my dear friend," answered

Puss. "It looks perfectly delicious to me."

"Never mind how it looks," said the retainer, overhearing Puss, Jr.'s, remark. "You must obey the law."

"I have no intention of not obeying," answered Puss, "nor would I endanger our safety by biting off a piece. Should the bridge fall into the water I should be forced to swim, and swimming is no easy matter for a cat, especially with high-top boots."

"Wisely said," replied the retainer. "And now that we have crossed over safely, I will leave you to pursue your journey, for you need no further help from me."

"Thank you," cried Puss, Jr.

"Yet there is one thing I would warn you of," replied the retainer, pausing before taking himself off. "In yonder forest is a gingerbread cottage. Beware of it, for within lives a wicked witch." With these words he turned away and crossed the gingerbread bridge that led back to Cranberry Tart Island.

"A gingerbread cottage," laughed Puss to himself, following the path that led into the forest:

"A gingerbread bridge

And a gingerbread house,

A gingerbread cat

And a gingerbread mouse.

But the gingerbread cat

Ate the gingerbread mouse

As she ran on the bridge

From the gingerbread house."

PUSS IN BOOTS, JR., VISITS THE OLD WOMAN IN THE SHOE

IT was now about high noon; but the air was cool and balmy, for the sun hardly penetrated the deep recesses of the green forest. As Puss trudged along he sang a little song to himself. I think he must have been something of a poet, for unconsciously his words rhymed and the air also was of his own making. A little brown wren, who was hopping along on the green moss that covered the floor of the great forest, heard him, and she told it to some one who afterward told it to me. And this is the way the little song went:

Through the woods, the cool woods,

The green woods, sweet with balm and fir,

To the music of the breeze

Singing softly through the trees

This the song I purr:—

Happy he who travels far,

Travels far and free,

Over valley, over hill,

Over smiling lea;

Never weary of the road,
Happy that he be
Just a jolly traveler
Wandering, like me!

As Puss finished his song he emerged from the woods and found himself upon a broad highway. "This must be the road that will lead me to my father's home," he said to himself, and joyfully proceeded on his journey.

OUT ON A LIMB, FROM WHICH HE DANGLED HIS RED-TOPPED BOOTS

In the distance he saw what looked like a queer little house, but as he drew nearer he saw it wasn't a house at all, but a big shoe. So many children were playing around, running in and out, that he would have found it difficult to count them, even if he had tried.

"Hello!" he called out to a little boy who was the only one who hadn't run into the shoe to tell mother that a big cat with boots on was coming up the garden walk.

"Hello!" Puss, Jr., said again, and the little fellow bashfully put out his hand.

"You have pretty boots," he said, looking down at them.

"Yes," answered their owner, "I'm rather proud of them myself; but what are your little brothers and sisters afraid of?" he added, as he noticed them peeking at him out of the window. "I won't hurt them."

Just then the Old Woman Who Lived in the Shoe came out, and, seeing one of her children talking to a strange cat who wore boots, she hurried up to them and asked:

"Are you Puss in Boots?"

"No, ma'am, but I'm his son," was the quick reply. "I'm Puss in Boots, Junior."

"Oh, of course," she said. "I knew your father years ago, and for a moment I forgot how time flies. Yes, we were very good friends in those old days. He was a very fine cat."

Puss, Jr., nodded politely.

"Won't you come in?" the Old Woman asked, turning toward her shoe house, "though you may find it difficult, as I can hardly find room for all my children. I suppose people think I'm very cross," she continued, as they managed to squeeze past the children in the hallway, "because I give them all a whipping before putting them to bed; but if I didn't, those I put to bed first wouldn't lie still. You see, by the time I get the last one to bed it's time to take the first one up for breakfast."

Puss, Jr., felt very sorry for her, as she didn't seem cross a bit, and the children clung to her skirt in a loving manner.

"Will you have a bowl of broth?" she asked. "It is about lunch-time, and I'm going to give the children some."

He thanked her, and said he would gladly, as he was hungry and tired. He sat down with the children, who had by this time arranged themselves in a row, each one with an empty bowl in his hands. The broth tasted very good, and Puss, Jr., felt so much better after eating it that he proposed a game of tag. They all ran outside and stood around in a ring while he counted "eeny, meeny, miney, mo," till all were out except himself.

"You're it!" the children cried, gleefully.

What a frolic followed! He finally caught the biggest boy, making believe for some time to miss the little tots, who screamed with fun as he chased them in and out among the trees.

It was a different matter, however, when it came to catch Puss, Jr. At last, with a jump, he ran up a tree and out on a limb, from which he dangled his red-topped boots over their heads. When every one gave up, he came down, and, after thanking the Old Woman for her kindness with a flourish and bow, he resumed his journey.

PUSS, JR., JOINS THE CIRCUS

A S Puss, Jr., neared a pretty village his attention was
attracted to a large tent in a field. Gaily colored wag-
ons were standing close by, and every now and then a roar
or a growl could be heard quite distinctly.

"A circus!" cried Puss, and he hastened forward and entered a small opening in the fence. As he approached the
great tent he heard a voice singing; it came from a little
side-tent. It was a woman's voice, quite soft and low:

"Oh, mother, I'm to be married

To Mr. Punchinello;

To Mr. Pun, to Mr. Chin, to

Mr. Nel, to Mr. Lo,

Mr. Pun, Mr. Chin, Mr. Nel, Mr. Lo,

To Mr. Punchinello."

As the last words died away a clown came from behind
a circus-wagon.

"Nello, Nello!" he called.

"What is it, Punch?" inquired the owner of the pretty
voice, appearing in the doorway of her tent. But before he
could answer she exclaimed: "Oh, look! See the cat with
red-topped boots!"

The clown turned and gazed at Puss, Jr., who came forward and put out his paw.

"Won't you join our circus?" said the clown, with an engaging smile.

Puss did not reply for a moment. He was thinking it over quite seriously. Whether or not it would interfere with his finding his father was the question. While he stood debating as to what was the thing to do, the circus-lady came out of her tent and cried:

"Oh, do join our circus, Sir Puss! I am sure you would be a great attraction. Every child in town would want to see a cat who wore boots!"

At this Puss, Jr.'s, face was all smiles. In fact, his whiskers curled up in a most laughable way, making his little face quite irresistible.

"Thank you both very much," he replied, "but before I answer I must tell you that I am in search of my illustrious parent, the famous Puss in Boots. If I join your circus how am I to find my dear father?"

"Easy as not," answered the clown, quickly. "We are always on the move. A new town 'most every day. We never linger long in any one spot."

"No, indeed, we don't!" cried the circus-lady. "We give a performance this afternoon and to-night, and then we pack up and are off again."

"You can have one of the circus-horses to ride," suggested the clown, by way of encouragement; "you need not travel on foot if you join us."

"That's a big inducement," admitted Puss, Jr.

"It's a merry life," added the circus-lady, "and when all the little children clap their hands and cry 'Bravo!' it's very exciting."

"I'll join," said Puss; "here's my paw!"

"And here's my hand," said the clown.

"And here's mine," cried the circus-lady.

"Come with me," said the clown, "and I'll put your name on the program and you shall be a regular circus performer from now on."

And that is how Puss, Jr., joined the circus.

PUSS, JR., PROVES TO BE A WONDERFUL CIRCUS PERFORMER

IT was about eight-thirty o'clock in the evening. The big tent was all aglow with lights. A long line of people reached from the dusty roadway to the ticket-office. Flaring torches threw strange streaks of light over the field, lighting up the circus-wagons with their gleaming red bodies and yellow wheels.

Now and then the roars of the lions and the trumpetings of the elephants could be heard, then the music of the band, a bugle-call, a shrill voice, a snap of whips—all the familiar sounds of a traveling circus, as the evening breeze ruffled the many flags that decked the great white tent. Puss, Jr., stood by the side of the clown in the tan-bark ring and looked about him. On all sides were eager faces. Hundreds of children screamed and yelled as the clown came forward and motioned for silence. When the sounds had died away he spoke, loud and clear:

"Ladies and gentlemen and little children, we have with us to-night the son of the famous Puss in Boots, the well-known nursery character, dearly loved by old and young. Puss, Junior, is in search of his father, but in the meantime has consented to join our circus. I venture to say that no other circus in the world has so wonderful a cat among its performers. You will all be charmed to see him act. His first performance will be to ride around the ring on our beautiful Arabian horse, White Marvel!" As the clown finished Puss jumped nimbly to the horse's back and commenced riding around the ring as if he had been accustomed to this sort of thing all his life.

The children clapped their hands, and the grown-ups smiled and nodded approvingly. The white horse broke into a gallop, but Puss stood first on one leg and then on the other, bowing gracefully here and there. Not once did he lose his balance, although he wore his red-topped boots, and to stand on the bare back of a horse under such conditions is not the easiest thing in the world.

When the clown brought out a wooden ring covered with tissue-paper the crowd held its breath. Would Puss, Jr., dare jump through it? Around galloped the big white horse in a swift canter, Puss balancing himself on one leg. As he neared the clown, who stood on a big blue barrel close to the ringside, Puss gathered himself together for the jump. Through the tissue-paper he went like a bird on the wing, and landed safely on the horse's back.

A wild round of applause greeted his daring deed. The children clapped their hands and screamed, forgetting in their excitement to eat their peanuts and candy popcorn. The man who carried the pink lemonade in funny little glasses all set in rows in a tin tray stood still to watch. He forgot to cry, "Anybody want some delicious, pink lemonade?" because he was so excited over the success of the new member of the circus family.

Then all the rest of the actor folk did their stunts; the monkeys played baseball, and the elephants had a boxing-match, and when all was over the clown and the circus-lady ran up to Puss, Jr., and said, "You were the star performer of the whole show!" which, of course, pleased Puss immensely.

A TERRIBLE FIGHT STOPPED
BY USING PLUM-CAKE

AS the circus entered a town one bright, sunny morning, the lion and the unicorn escaped from their cages. Great was the excitement! All the circus people started after them with long ropes, hoping to be able to lasso them.

At first the townsfolk were greatly frightened, but gradually, as they found out that the lion and the unicorn paid little attention to them, their fear gave way to interest. It seems that the lion was an enemy of the unicorn, and as soon as they were free they began to fight.

The Lion and the Unicorn were fighting for the crown,

The Lion beat the Unicorn all around the town.

Some gave them white bread, and some gave them brown,

Some gave them plum-cake and sent them out of town.

If it had not been for the plum-cake I verily believe they would have been fighting still. But as soon as the unicorn saw the plum-cake he said to the lion:

"What's the use of fighting, Leon? Let's have a truce. In fact, I'm hungry."

"So am I," replied the lion. "I haven't had a sweet thing since I joined the circus. And you know how hard it is to see all the little boys and girls eating candy and popcorn and not be able to get even one little piece."

"That's quite true," replied the unicorn. "People seem to think all I require is hay. And as for you, they think raw meat is enough."

With these friendly words they stopped fighting and began to eat the plum-cake. All the townsfolk stood by watching them. When the circus-men arrived on the scene they were too surprised for the moment to do a thing. They just stood still and watched the two animals eat the cake, even waiting until the lion had picked up the last crumb and the unicorn the last raisin. Then they came forward very quietly and threw a rope first over the lion's head and then over the unicorn's, and led them back to their cages. Puss, Jr., who had by this time arrived on the scene, turned to the people and said:

"Ladies and gentlemen, it was very kind of you to give plum-cake to our animals. It only goes to show what kindness will do. I hope you will appreciate how much we thank you for what you have done, and also that you will come to our show to-night. I can assure you we will give you a double bill to show you how much we appreciate what you have done for us."

"Hurrah!" cried the crowd. "Three cheers for Sir Cat!"

That night there was a tremendous attendance. The tent was crowded. Everybody was in a jolly frame of mind. All the circus people did their best. Puss, Jr., jumped through three hoops without touching the back of the big white horse, and the clown was funnier than he had ever been in all his life. The circus-lady never looked so pretty, nor did she ever ride so well before. And it took the ticket-seller all night to count the money.

PUSS, JR., MEETS ANOTHER CAT AND MORALIZES ON CONTENTMENT

FOR some time Puss, Jr., traveled with the circus, but at last, finding that he could make better time if he traveled alone, he said good-by and started off by himself. Perhaps he remembered the old saying, "He travels faster who travels alone." At any rate, he made up his mind on this point and set bravely out by himself.

But he was not lonely, for he was continually seeing new sights and new people.

One morning as he trudged along a road bordered by green meadows he saw at some little distance ahead a large apple-tree. As he drew near a pussy-cat ran up the trunk.

Little Robin Redbreast sat upon a tree,

Up went Pussy-Cat, and down went he;

Down came Pussy-Cat, away Robin ran;

Said Little Robin Redbreast, "Catch me if you can!"

Little Robin Redbreast jumped upon a wall,

Pussy-Cat jumped after him, and almost got a fall;

Little Robin chirp'd and sang, and what did Pussy say?

Pussy-Cat said, "Mew," and Robin flew away.

"What are you trying to do?" asked Puss in Boots, Jr., stopping in front of the tree and looking up at the pussy-cat, who sat upon the wall, looking after the robin, who had flown away.

"I'm not trying to do anything," replied the pussy-cat, crossly, "but I was wishing I had wings."

"They would be very nice," replied Puss, Jr., reflectively; "they would be most convenient at times."

"Indeed they would!" answered the pussy-cat; "they'd be lots better even than red-topped boots."

Puss looked down at his feet. "Perhaps," he answered, "but I have found my boots most helpful. Do you know," he continued, "if people would be a little more contented with what they have I think they'd get more."

The pussy-cat did not answer for a few minutes. Then she said: "What you say is very true. I suppose I ought to be thankful that I have such nice strong claws. It's not hard work climbing trees, and, as far as running goes, my legs carry me very well. Perhaps I don't need wings, after all."

"Well, I never saw a flying cat," admitted Puss, Jr., "although I've seen some remarkable things since I started out to find my father, Puss in Boots."

"So you are a traveler," said the pussy-cat, jumping down from the wall and walking up to Puss. "How long have you been seeking your father?"

"A long, long time," replied Puss, Jr. "Do you know, sometimes I almost get discouraged, for this is a big world and at times I feel so very, very small."

"Well, you come home with me," said the pussy-cat, "and get a good rest. I think you're tired out." This was the truth, for he had traveled far that day.

PUSS MEETS MOTHER GOOSE

O h, my pretty cock, oh, my handsome cock,
    I pray you do not crow before day,
And your comb shall be made of the very beaten gold,
And your wings of the silver so gray."

Puss, Jr., opened his eyes sleepily to find himself in Mother Goose's arms. They were seated on a gander's back, who was flying along as if such a thing as traveling with two passengers was nothing at all. As Mother Goose finished her little verse, the gander alighted on the roof of a big red barn on which a weathercock sedately turned this way and that in the early morning breeze. The sun was just coming up, for it was early, very early. Puss rubbed his eyes and sat up. "And how's my little pussy-cat?" asked Mother Goose, stroking him kindly. "Did he have a good night's sleep?"

"Yes, indeed, thank you," answered Puss, now thoroughly awake and remembering how he had met Mother Goose the previous day, and how fortunate it was that she had agreed to take him back to Mother Goose Land.

"Cock-a-doodle-do!" said the weathercock.

"Crow as much as you like," said Mother Goose. "Now that Puss is awake you can make all the noise you wish. At first I thought we were not going to stop on your barn, Sir Chantecler, and that was the reason I asked you to delay your early morning crow so that we could be far away before you commenced. Puss is in need of all the sleep he can get, for in a few days he will be on his feet again. He has still a long ways to go ere he finds his famous father, Puss in Boots."

"Well," answered the weathercock, "I didn't crow before day, so kindly give me a gold comb and silver wings."

"That I will," answered Mother Goose, "this very evening."

"And who will bring them?" asked the weathercock, for he was very vain, and is sometimes called a weather-vane, perhaps for that reason. "Who will bring them to me, and how am I to know that a gold comb will be becoming or that silver wings will suit my complexion?"

"Leave that to me," said Mother Goose, with a lofty air. "Weathercocks only know of the breezes that blow; they swing back and forth when the wind's from the north, the south, east or west—they are never at rest."

"More poetry from Mother Goose," sighed the weathercock. "If people must talk, why do they want to rhyme it out? Let them talk in good old prose. It suits me best."

Mother Goose evidently did not hear his remarks, for she was busily feeding the gander. Puss was stretching his legs by walking along the roof and watching some sparrows who were chirping under the eaves. Presently she called Puss. "We are off again," she cried; "get aboard the goose-ship!" When they were comfortably seated she turned to the weathercock and said: "This evening the sun will gild your comb and silver your wings just before he goes behind yonder western hill. Good-by!"

The weathercock did not reply, and the gander did not wait, but flew away with his two passengers safely sitting on his back.

TRIPPING WITH THE STARS

Twinkle, twinkle, little star,
How I wonder what you are!
Up above the world so high,
Like a diamond in the sky."

Puss repeated this little rhyme to himself as he looked at a lovely star that shone in the heavens with a soft and silvery light.

"I always liked that little song," said Mother Goose. "I've heard it time and again. Mothers always sing that to their babies just before they go to sleep."

"Do they?" asked Puss. "Mine never did. She used to sing about little mice and birds."

Mother Goose laughed heartily. "It all depends on whose little baby you are," she said, "but I guess it all comes out all right in the end."

The gander said never a word. He was doubtless too busy propelling his great wings and steering with his tail to pay much attention to what his two passengers were saying.

I don't know whether there was a sign up like the ones

they have in the cars, "Don't talk to the motorman," or not. At any rate, the gander observed the law, for he made no answer. On and on they went, through the night. Past cloud and star, over river and valley, hill and dale, swiftly and silently, for after these few remarks both Mother Goose and Puss grew very sleepy.

It must have been well on toward morning before they awoke. Nestled on a soft, feathery gander's back, with the wind singing lullabies as you travel swiftly underneath the stars, is quite sufficient to keep any one asleep. It was indeed a mighty fine cradle, and if the morning sun had not poked his golden fingers into Puss, Jr.'s, eyes he might still have been sound asleep.

"Mother Goose," he cried, touching the dear old lady gently on the shoulder, "we are getting very near the earth. It's time for you to wake up."

"To be sure it is," she replied, rubbing her eyes and arranging her curls beneath her old peaked hat; "to be sure, and, dearie me! I believe I have actually overslept!"

They were now close to the earth. The cocks were crowing lustily in the barn-yards, and every now and then the bark of a dog, faint but clear, would come to their ears.

"It's funny to look at a house from the outside in the early morning," said Puss. "I've always looked out from the inside."

"Of course you have, my dear little traveler," answered Mother Goose, "but now that you are on your journey to find your famous father, Puss in Boots, you will see many things very differently."

"Well," said the gander, for the first time speaking, "I'm a bit tired, so I think I will alight near this old barn."

Puss was delighted, for he wanted once more to feel himself on earth.

PUSS FINDS ADVENTURE AT THE TOP OF JACK'S FAMOUS BEAN-STALK

THE next morning as Puss, Jr., went journeying along he came in sight of a modest little cottage, in the garden of which was growing an immense bean-stalk, reaching up and up until its top was hidden in the clouds. On approaching the front gate, a motherly-looking woman appeared in the doorway and looked curiously at Puss.

"Good morning, ma'am," said he, lifting his cap politely.

"Good morning," she replied, at the same time wiping a tear from her eyes. "Have you seen anything of my son Jack?"

"No, ma'am," answered Puss. "Has he not yet climbed down the bean-stalk?"

"What!" exclaimed the good woman. "Do you mean to tell me he has climbed up this giant bean-stalk?"

"Indeed he has," answered Puss, "and if you will permit me I will climb up also. Maybe I shall find him near the top, or possibly entangled in the vines."

The good woman gladly gave her consent and Puss

sprang nimbly up the vine-like ladder. Up and up he climbed until he was lost to sight amid the white clouds in the sky. At last he reached the top, and, looking about him curiously, wondered which way to turn. Suddenly he heard a gentle cackling near at hand, and a small hen crawled out of a thicket that lay to the right of the path.

"I'm tired to death laying golden eggs for that greedy giant,

"To lay every day

Is all work and no play,"

"GOOD MORNING, MA'AM," SAID HE, LIFTING HIS CAP POLITELY

she continued, unconsciously making a little rhyme.

"But where is Jack?" asked Puss, after he had consoled her by saying that there was much harder work in the world than laying golden eggs.

"Oh, he's up at the giant's house, hiding somewhere," she replied.

"Won't you show me the way?" said Puss, "for I have a message from his mother to deliver to him."

"Come along; follow me," she cackled, and Puss walked by her side, politely helping her over the rough places, as the path became steeper and steeper. Near the top of the hill was the giant's house. But Puss was not afraid and boldly followed the little hen through the great doorway and presently found himself in the presence of the giant.

"GOOD MORNING, MA'AM," SAID HE, LIFTING HIS CAP POLITELY

"Come, chick," cried the giant, not noticing Puss. "Come, chick, and lay me a gold egg!"

"I'm so tired to-day," she replied, "won't you let me off just for once?"

"No, siree!" roared the giant. "Lay! lay!"

"How dare you be so cruel, Sir Giant!" roared Puss as loud as he could, stepping forward and brandishing his staff.

"Heighty tighty!" laughed the giant, "on one condition will I let off the little hen, and that is that you spend the night in my house and tell me some of your adventures."

Puss, Jr., bowed low and graciously. He was able now to reward the little hen for showing him the way, and as the guest of the giant, it would be much easier to find Jack. Puss made up his mind toward midnight to hunt over the entire house for him.

PUSS DISCOVERS WHERE JACK IS HIDING

PUSS, JR., found the giant a very agreeable host. Perhaps it was because Puss told so many interesting stories of what he had seen and done since leaving the garret.

"By the time you find your father," roared the giant, for even when he whispered it sounded like thunder, "you will have traveled far and wide, my dear friend."

They were seated in the giant's great living-room. A huge pipe was in his mouth, the smoke from which rose in a cloud as big as that from a factory chimney. Puss, Jr., was not the least bit dismayed, however, for he was naturally a brave cat, and his many adventures had given him an air of assurance as well as a liberal education. He sat opposite the giant and recounted his adventures one after another, much to the delight of his great host. All the while, however, Puss was scheming as to the best way to discover Jack. He had made up his mind firmly that after his long climb up the bean-stalk, and the fact that he had been so lucky as to make a friend of the giant, he would allow nothing to turn him aside.

Finally the giant fell sound asleep. Puss carefully opened

the door and tiptoed into the kitchen, where the giant's wife was washing up the supper-dishes. As he entered he noticed that the oven door was open just a crack. "My good woman," said Puss, "your husband is asleep, so I have taken this opportunity to thank you for the very fine supper of which I have just partaken."

The giant's wife started at the sound of his voice and immediately walked over and stood in front of the oven as if to guard it from view.

"Ha, ha!" said Puss to himself. "I'll wager Jack is in the oven. I wonder why the good woman mistrusts me.

"Madam," said Puss, "I'm in search of a little boy named Jack, and I have a message from his mother for him. Jack of the wonderful bean-stalk, and I am sure he is in yonder oven."

Puss, Jr., heard a scratching sound, then a creak, and in a moment Jack stepped from behind the giant's wife, after carefully closing the oven door.

"How do you do," said Jack, coming forward, "and what does mother want?"

"She is worried about you," replied Puss, Jr., "and asked me to tell you, should I have the good fortune of meeting you, that she hoped you would return home, for she is so lonely."

"That I will," answered Jack, "as soon as I have the opportunity." He had hardly finished speaking when the heavy tread of the giant was heard. Jack jumped back into the oven, while the giant's wife commenced talking to Puss, Jr., as if nothing whatever had happened.

"Why did you leave me?" roared the giant, turning fiercely to Puss.

"Why did you fall asleep?" asked Puss. "Were my tales not of sufficient interest to keep you awake?"

"They were," replied the giant, somewhat taken aback by the answer he received. "I guess I have the habit of falling asleep after supper. It's mighty difficult to break a habit."

"It is, indeed," said Puss. "I feel sleepy myself. Will you allow me not to break my habit of going to bed early?"

The giant laughed long and loud. "Show him his room, mother," he said, turning to his wife. So Puss said good night and followed her up-stairs, having made up his mind to meet Jack at midnight.

PUSS AND JACK MAKE A BOLD RESCUE

IT was midnight in the giant's house. Puss Jr., heard the great clock strike twelve. Softly he tiptoed down the stairs, holding his boots in one paw and his staff and cap in the other. When he reached the great living-room he peeped cautiously in.

There sat the giant in the big arm-chair, fast asleep, the poor little hen that laid the golden eggs lying on the table, not daring to move.

"How dare he break his word?" said Puss to himself. "He promised if I told him stories last night that he would not make the little hen lay her daily golden egg. Now he has gone and broken his promise."

The little hen moved uneasily and looked appealingly at Puss.

"What can I do?" he said to himself. Suddenly a bright idea came into his head, and, turning toward the kitchen, he opened the door very softly and peered in. To his great delight he saw Jack sound asleep in the big rocking-chair that the giant's wife sat in during the few moments of the day in which she was not hard at work. Puss, Jr., carefully set his boots down near the door and walked over to Jack. Fearing he might let out a cry of surprise upon seeing him, Puss paused.

"How shall I waken him without startling him?" he asked himself. It was indeed a problem. Should Jack give a scream the giant would wake and rush in. Then all would be lost. It was a trying moment for Puss, Jr.

Suddenly an owl hooted outside. Jack slowly opened his eyes.

"'S-sh!" cautioned Puss, quietly, "be careful!"

"Don't worry," replied Jack in a whisper. "I've no desire to make the acquaintance of the giant. He wouldn't care for my stories. He'd just eat me up."

"That he would," said Puss. "He's no good, either. He broke his promise to me last night," and then Puss told Jack how the giant had said he would let the little hen off for once if Puss would tell some of his adventures.

"And I spent all last evening telling him stories till I was tired out," concluded Puss, "and now he has kept that poor little hen by his side all night long. She's in the great living-room on the table, not daring to move. And the giant has the gold egg tightly grasped in his hand."

"Let's rescue the little hen," said Puss.

"How can we?" asked Jack.

"Why, just run off with her," replied Puss.

"Where to?" said Jack, for he was still rather sleepy and his mind was not working as rapidly as Puss, Jr.'s.

"Take her home to your mother," whispered Puss. Together they crept into the room where the giant still lay snoring. Jack carefully picked up the little hen and started for the door. As he did so he knocked Puss, Jr.'s, staff from his paw.

"Run!" cried Puss, as the giant opened his eyes. They fell upon Puss, for Jack had disappeared down the bean-stalk.

"You have stolen my hen!" he roared.

Puss darted in another direction and the giant after him. Just then the little owl, who had awakened Jack, flew near and called out:

"The Owl and the Pussy-Cat went to sea

In a beautiful pea-green boat."

And this is the way Puss, Jr., escaped from the wicked giant.

PUSS, JR., MEETS MR. ROWLEY FROG

THE following day Puss, Jr., was trudging along near the edge of a forest. The land was rather low and marshy, and the path was none too dry. He gingerly picked his way, avoiding as well as possible the muddy spots. Of a sudden his attention was arrested by a funny sight.

A few feet in front of him, as he rounded a curve in the path, was a frog. On his head rested a large stove-pipe hat, much worn and weather-beaten. A large cigar was in his mouth, on which he puffed away vigorously, the clouds of smoke streaming out behind him like a long gray feather.

"Hello, Mr. Rowley!" cried Puss.

The frog turned. Taking the cigar out of his mouth, he answered, "How do you know my name?"

"Just a good guess of mine, perhaps," replied Puss. "But, anyway, there's a famous Mr. Rowley in Mother Goose, so I took a chance."

"Well, I don't want you to try to stop me," said Rowley, "for I had enough fuss when I left home. You see, my people didn't want me to go at all."

"Then why did you?" asked Puss, who by this time had come up to the frog.

"Because I was tired to death of the old pond," replied

Rowley. "One has got to see the world some time, and when one is young is the time and not when one is old."

"Yes, 'every dog must have his day,'" quoted Puss.

"And every frog, too," answered Rowley, pushing his high hat down on his head more securely and replacing the cigar between his lips.

"And where are you going?" asked Puss.

"A frog he would a-wooing go,

Heigh-ho! says Rowley.

Whether his mother would let him or no.

With a rowley powley, gammon and spinach,

Heigh-ho! says Anthony Rowley."

"Well, then, Anthony!" cried Puss, taking the frog by the arm, "let us be comrades. For it is lonesome business, this traveling alone, and I would have a good friend to talk to while we trudge along."

"But I already have a companion," answered Mr. Rowley. "Don't you remember the second verse in Mother Goose?"

"Not exactly," replied Puss, Jr.

"Well, this is the way it goes," answered the frog. "It's describing me, of course."

"So off he set with his opera hat,

Heigh-ho! says Rowley.

And on the road he met with a rat.

'Pray, Mr. Rat, will you go with me?'

Heigh-ho! says Rowley,

'Kind Mrs. Mousey for to see?'"

At that moment the rat jumped out of the bushes. "Don't be afraid," said Puss, Jr.

"All right," replied the rat, "I sha'n't."

"Glad to have seen you both," said Puss, Jr. "I can't tarry long, for I must continue my journey."

PUSS IS HEARTILY WELCOMED BY JACK THE JUMPER

IT was near nightfall. Puss, Jr., was weary and footsore, for he had traveled far. No one had given him a thing to eat all day, and he was faint from want of food. Darkness was coming upon him and he looked about him to find a place to sleep.

In the distance a little light caught his eye, and, hastening his steps toward it, he soon came to a small cottage. Looking through the open door, he was surprised to see resting on the floor a small brass candlestick. It was the flame from this that had attracted his attention and drawn his weary feet forward.

Jack be nimble,

Jack be quick,

And Jack jump over the candlestick.

Over the candlestick leaped a small boy, and with a laugh turned toward the open door.

"Can you jump over a lighted candlestick?" he asked.

"I never tried," said Puss, "but I guess I can."

"Don't singe your tail!" cried Jack, as Puss prepared himself for the jump.

"Don't worry," replied Puss, Jr. "I think too much of my tail to spoil one single little hair."

Gathering himself together, Puss jumped nimbly over the candle.

"Good for you!" cried the little boy.

"Oh, that's nothing," replied Puss. "I once belonged to a circus."

"You did?" cried the little boy. "Tell me about it."

"Well," said Puss, "there isn't much to tell. I was walking along one day and came up to a big tent. A man asked me if I would not like to join, and I said yes."

"What did you do?" asked the little boy.

"Oh, I rode a horse around the ring. I jumped through hoops covered with tissue-paper, and I never slipped off. It was pretty good fun," sighed Puss, Jr. "But, dear me, I'm so hungry! Can't you get me some milk?"

"Of course I can," replied the little boy; "you just sit down and see that the candle doesn't blow out, and I'll run and tell mother." In a few minutes he returned, followed by a motherly-looking woman.

"Why, it's Puss in Boots!" she said.

"No, madam," replied Puss; "but I'm his son, and have been these many months trying to find my dear father."

"And you haven't found him yet?" said the good woman.

"No, not yet," replied our little hero, "but I hope to very soon."

"Well, you shall have a good supper," said the kind woman, "for my little boy tells me you are hungry."

In a few minutes Puss was eating a hearty supper, and then he followed the little boy up to his bedroom, where they both slept soundly all night long after mother had blown out the light.

OLD KING COLE'S FIDDLERS ARE RATHER RUDE TO PUSS

OLD King Cole was a merry old soul,
And a merry old soul was he;
And he called for his pipe,
And he called for his bowl,
And he called for his fiddlers three.
And every fiddler, he had a fine fiddle,
And a very fine fiddle had he;
"Tweedle dee, tweedle dee," said the fiddlers;
"Oh, there's none so rare as can compare,
With Old King Cole and his fiddlers three."

Cole Castle was a very magnificent one. Puss looked up at the great walls and sighed. "I wish I would find my dear father here, but I suppose I won't."

"No, you won't," cried a voice, and one of the three fiddlers poked his head out of a window and laughed loud and long. "There are no cats in this castle."

"No cats allowed here," cried the third fiddler, appearing at the postern gate.

Puss, Jr., almost felt like crying. "Did you ever hear of Puss in Boots?" he asked.

"Certainly," replied all three fiddlers at once, "but he doesn't live here. No cats do. We make all the noise in this castle. You don't think for a moment Old King Cole could stand any more noise, do you?"

"My father wouldn't make any noise," replied Puss, Jr., indignantly.

"I never heard of a cat that didn't," said one of the fiddlers.

"All cats make an awful noise at night," said another.

"They meow and cry like everything on the back fence," said the third fiddler. "They make more noise than a fiddle, and a worse noise than a fiddle out of tune."

"I don't like you," said Puss. "People who don't like cats are not to be trusted."

"Ha, ha!" laughed all three fiddlers, "you're jealous of us!"

"Not the least," replied Puss, stoutly. "I'm not jealous at all. I'm just indignant that you should make such a remark about my family."

"No harm meant," said the three fiddlers, "no harm meant, my good Sir Cat."

"Very well, we won't argue the matter," said Puss, "for a traveler has no time to argue if he would reach his journey's end. Time is precious, and I must be on my way. Only let me tell you, I have heard many a fiddle that made a worse noise than a cat," and with this parting remark our little hero continued on his way.

THE MILLER OF THE DEE

WHAT a lovely old mill!" thought Puss, Jr. "Is that your 'hush-a-by baby upon the tree-top'?" he asked the miller on entering the old mill.

"No, sir-ee!" answered the jolly miller, with a jolly laugh. "Haven't you ever heard the song about me? This is the way it goes:

"There was a jolly miller once

Lived on the River Dee;

He worked and sang from morn till night,

No lark so blithe as he.

"And this the burden of his song

Forever used to be:

'I care for nobody! No, not I!

And nobody cares for me!'"

"Doesn't anybody care for you?" asked Puss. "It seems strange, for you are so jolly."

"Well," answered the miller, "you see, it's this way: I am here all alone all day; there's no room in the mill except for me and the sacks of corn. It all belongs to me, even the old willow-tree. I let a little woman who lives quite near here

"AREN'T WE GREAT FRIENDS?" ASKED THE MILLER

hang the cradle on the limb every morning. As she goes to work in the village, she puts her baby in the cradle and the wind rocks it to sleep until she comes back at noon. Then she goes away again and comes back at evening and takes the cradle home with her. The baby is very good; that is, it has been so far; but you can never tell how long a baby will be good."

"That's true of every one," said Puss, with much gravity.

"If it ever starts crying—that is, a long crying spell, she'll have to get another willow-tree or another baby. I can't be bothered with a crying baby so close at hand."

"But you haven't answered my question yet," said Puss.

"Oh," replied the miller. "You mean because I care for nobody and nobody cares for me."

"Yes; I don't quite understand it."

"Come inside and I'll explain it to you," said the miller.

Puss walked inside and sat down on a bag of flour. "All I do is to grind corn for people," continued the miller, sitting down on a dusty stool. "They bring their corn in to be ground and then they leave. When they come back the corn is ready for them,—that is, the flour. They take it away and I'm left all alone. So what do I do? Well, I make friends with a little mouse and a big rat that live in the old mill." As he spoke the little mouse ran out of her hole and sat down by the miller. "We are great friends, aren't we, mousie?" he said.

The little mouse squeaked, "Yes, Mr. Miller."

Then the big rat came out and sat down by the miller, only on the other side.

"Aren't we great friends?" asked the miller.

The rat said, "You are the best friend I have." At which the miller smiled and Puss grinned.

"Animals make good friends," said the miller.

"Yes, indeed," replied Puss, "but rats and mice are so destructive. They eat your corn."

"Not much," said the miller; "only a little bit."

"We only eat what we need," said the mouse and the rat in chorus.

PUSS, JR., RENDERS A MOTHER AID

PUSS, JR., was very much interested in the jolly miller and his two small friends, the rat and the mouse. It seemed strange to Puss that a miller should have two such friends as these. But when he thought it over he saw there was much reason to the miller's words.

At the time the miller was talking the mouse and the rat kept a close watch on Puss, Jr. They knew from experience, most likely, that cats are not millers, and although Puss, Jr., with his boots and cap, his clothes and staff, did not resemble an ordinary cat, at the same time he was a cat. So the rat and the mouse kept at a safe distance.

"Tell your little friends," said Puss to the jolly miller, "that I won't hurt a hair of them."

"Mousie," said the miller, leaning over and patting the little mouse, "Sir Cat says he will not harm a hair of your tiny head."

"That's very kind of him," replied the little mouse in a squeaky voice.

The rat made the same answer when the miller patted him.

Just then the mother of the baby who was in the cradle on the tree-top came by. She smiled at the miller, who took off his rusty, dusty cap. "There she goes," he said to Puss. "She's going to take the cradle down now. She'll take 'cradle, and baby, and all' home with her."

Puss stepped to the doorway to watch her. First she stood on tiptoe and looked into the cradle. Then she smiled and leaned over and kissed the baby, who began to crow and clap his hands. After she had kissed him many times she lifted him out of the cradle and danced him up and down on her knee. As she danced him gently up and down, she sang:

"Down in the village, all the day long,

Mother's been singing a sweet little song;

Just to herself she's been singing all day,

While baby's been rocking and rocking away:

'Hush-a-by, baby, upon the tree-top,

Mother is watching the tick-tocky clock;

Counting the minutes go by until she

Will be taking her baby boy down from the tree.'"

Then she laid the baby over her shoulder and, picking up the cradle, started off for home.

"Let me carry the cradle for you," said Puss, Jr., running out of the mill.

"That would be a great help," she replied, "for baby is getting very heavy, and mother has been working hard all day."

So Puss put the cradle on his shoulder and, bowing to the miller, followed after her, while the baby kicked and crowed and tried to reach down and pull his whiskers. And Puss tickled the baby's hand and winked at the baby, who gurgled and laughed and tried to pull the feather out of Puss, Jr.'s, cap. And the little mother forgot all about her own weariness, for baby lay so warm against her neck and his laugh tinkled so sweetly in her ear!

THE MILKMAN'S HORSE, OLD NAGGETTY NOGG

Jockety jog, jockety jog!
   Over the hills, and over the bog.
"Jockety jog, jockety jog!
Many a mile this day I've trod.
"Jockety jog, jockety jog!
I'm the milkman's horse, old Naggetty Nogg."

"Are you really?" exclaimed Puss, Jr., looking up into the face of the old white horse. "And is your name 'Naggetty Nogg'?"

"Yes, that's my name," replied the old horse. "You see, every horse is a nag. So in some way or another they got to calling me 'Naggetty,' and then, after a while, they added on the 'Nogg.'"

"Yes, every one has at least two names," replied Puss, "and it is natural that you should have two, just like everybody. I like the name 'Naggetty Nogg' very much. It's quite fine."

"It sounds 'horsy' all right," he answered, giving his tail a sweep to brush off some flies that had settled on his side. "It sounds real horsy."

"And it fits you perfectly," said Puss. "You couldn't have chosen a better name."

"But I didn't choose it," replied the old horse, quickly; "it was given to me. You see, my master and I start out early every morning. First we go to the farm to get the milk. It's so early in the morning that it's quite dark sometimes—that is, in the winter-time. The farmer comes out and opens the milk-house door with his key. The milk is all kept in great big pans in long rows. It's very cool inside, for the milk-house is built over a spring that bubbles away all the time, running out of the old stone milk-house down to the meadows, where the cows drink it and the little fish swim in it. I know, because one time when my right forefoot was hurt they put me out in the meadow and many a good drink I've had from that same little brook. The bottom is all bright little stones, and the ferns hang over the edge of the bank, and the little birds hop down and drink. Oh, it's very pleasant out there in the meadow. I sometimes wish my old foot would go lame again so that I might enjoy the green grass and the cool breezes. But that wouldn't do at all. My master would lose money. He would have to hire another horse. And then, too, I would miss the mothers who come out to get the nice fresh milk from my master. Sometimes they have a baby in their arms and two or three small children hanging on to their skirts. And they always pat my nose and say:

"'How is old Naggetty Nogg to-day?' Sometimes I get a lump of sugar, too."

"You make me wish that I could drive a milk-wagon," said Puss, Jr., with a sigh. "I'd like to be a milkman if I had a Naggetty Nogg to drive."

WHO IS A MAN'S MOST FAITHFUL FRIEND?

WHAT is your master's name?" asked Puss, Jr., as the old white milk-horse paused in his story.

"Jockety jog, jockety jog!

My master's name is Roundey K. Rogg.

"Jockety jog, jockety jog!

He's a good man; he drinks no grog.

"Jockety jog, jockety jog!

Never does he old Naggetty flog."

"That's a blessing," said Puss, Jr. "I've seen so many poor horses whipped. It's a shame that a man can hurt a horse."

"Yes, a horse is a man's most faithful friend," replied old Naggetty. "He works for him all the time."

"Don't you get tired?" asked Puss.

"No-o-o," replied the old horse, "not very tired. You see, when we start out we have the cans full. So we go very slowly so as not to churn the milk or spill it. If we went too fast the tops of the cans might fly off. Then on our way home, when all the milk has been delivered and all the hungry little children have had all they can drink, we come along at a good clip. The cans bump and make a most cheerful noise. And every step is nearer home, where my supper of oats is waiting for me, and my good master's supper is waiting for him."

"I'd like to climb up into your wagon and go home with you," said Puss. "Do you suppose your master would object?"

"You can ask him," replied the old horse. "But you mustn't climb up until you do."

"Certainly not," replied Puss, indignantly. "I wouldn't take such a liberty. Tell me more about him." The old horse whisked his tail and commenced:

"Jockety jog, jockety jog!

I'll bear him safe through all this fog.

"Jockety jog, jockety jog!

How the darkness this way doth clog."

The old horse paused. "I was thinking of a dark night some time ago. The moon was hidden behind the clouds and not a star was to be seen. We had gone a long ways out of our usual track, for my master had heard of a poor woman who had a sick baby, and he said he must take her some fresh milk. When we started back for home it was already pretty dark, but I knew the road. My master left it all to me. He just let the reins hang down over the dashboard and gave me my head. So I kept along, taking good care not to stumble. The tin cans bumped and banged together and the wheels creaked over the rough places. Master began to sing his favorite song:

"Place the little candle-light

In the window clear and bright.

Tho' the night be dim and dark

I shall see its tiny spark."

PUSS BUYS A PAIR OF BOOTS MADE FOR HIS FAMOUS SIRE

S OLOMON Grundy,
　　Born on a Monday,
Christened on Tuesday,
Married on Wednesday,
Took ill on Thursday,
Worse on Friday,
Died on Saturday,
Buried on Sunday.
This is the end of
Solomon Grundy.

Puss, Jr., stood before a little shop. In the window was this sign. "Too bad," said Puss to himself; "he had such a nice little store."

"He did that!" cried a voice. Puss looked up and saw a little old woman. On her head was a queer green bonnet and over her shoulders hung a faded red shawl. "Are you Mrs. Grundy?" asked Puss. For some reason he felt sure it was, so he was not at all surprised when she answered yes.

"And do you still run the little shop?" he asked.

"Yes, my good Sir Cat," she replied, "and I have a very fine pair of red-topped boots which I would like to sell you."

"I guess I need a new pair," said Puss, Jr., looking down at his own. There was a big hole in the toe of one and the other was minus a heel.

"Walk in," said little old Mrs. Grundy, "and you may try them on." Puss followed her into the store and sat down. Mrs. Grundy climbed up a little step-ladder and took down a box from the top shelf. "This pair of boots," she said, "was made once upon a time, very long ago, for a very famous cat whose name was Puss in Boots."

At these words Puss, Jr., jumped off his seat and threw his paws around Mrs. Grundy.

"Gracious me!" she cried, "what are you doing?"

"Oh, my dear madam," cried Puss, "the famous cat you mention is my father—I am Puss in Boots, Junior."

"Is that possible?" exclaimed Mrs. Grundy, letting the box fall with a bang to the floor. "Is that possible? I'm so glad that I saved these boots all these years. And to think that his son will wear them," she added, sitting down in her excitement.

"But I don't care much about the boots!" cried Puss, Jr. "I want so badly to find my father. Can't you tell me where he lives?"

Mrs. Grundy looked puzzled. "I did know, my little friend," she replied, "but I have clean forgotten now. Indeed I have," she added, in a sympathetic voice, seeing how disappointed poor little Puss looked.

"Just the same, I will pay you well for the boots," said Puss, Jr., "and be on my way at once. One never can tell what each day may bring, and I might find my father, although it grieves me to think you have forgotten just where he lives."

PUSS MEETS A MODEST MENDING MAN AND A JOLLY MILLER

IF I'd as much money as I could spend
   I never would cry old chairs to mend;
Old chairs to mend, old chairs to mend,
I never would cry old chairs to mend.
"If I'd as much money as I could tell,
I never would cry old clothes to sell;
Old clothes to sell, old clothes to sell,
I never would cry old clothes to sell."

"Well, what would you do?" asked Puss, Jr., coming up to the funny little man who was singing this song as he journeyed along over the roadway down the hill, across the bridge to the creaking mill.

"I'd buy a little house and a little cow and a little pig, and I'd live all the days of my life as happy as could be," replied the funny little man.

"That wouldn't take such an awful lot of money," replied Puss. "You said in your song if you had 'as much money as you could spend.' I should think that would mean a big castle and a big automobile and a big yacht, and, and—"

"I couldn't spend more than a little, for I've never had much practice in spending," answered the funny little man.

Before Puss could make reply they crossed the bridge and found themselves opposite the old mill. In the doorway stood the miller all covered with flour. His hat was dusty, too; even his hair and eyelashes were white with the dusty flour.

"IF I'D AS MUCH MONEY AS I COULD SPEND"

"Any old chairs to mend?" asked the funny little man.

"I have a stool here that has lost a leg," replied the miller, "and an old clock that has lost a hand, and my wife has a pitcher that has lost a mouth and a needle that has no eye. Can you mend them all?"

"You'd better call in the doctor," said the funny little man; "he's the person you want."

"Ha, ha!" roared the miller, "I was only joking."

"So was I," answered the little man. "Give me the stool. I will heal that patient first, then will see about the others."

The miller presently brought out the injured stool, and while it was being mended he and Puss, Jr., had a talk.

"Yes," said the miller as Puss seated himself on a sack of flour, "I'm a busy man. It's grind, grind all day long. Red corn and yellow corn and white corn from the cribs of the farmers. From the fields to my mill, and then from here to the baker or the kitchen, and then into cakes for little children. The big wheel goes round and round all day long and the water splashes and gurgles as it turns it. And then I tie up the sacks after they are well filled, and then the wagon comes and takes them away. Every day the same thing, year in and year out."

"It's nice and cool," said Puss, "and the flour smells sweet, and it's home, you know. I'm a little tired with my long journey and wish I could find my dear father."

"Cheer up," said the miller. "You'll find him soon, I'm sure of that."

PUSS OVERHEARS A PROPOSAL AND IS INVITED TO A WEDDING

IT was a merry time,
    When Jenny Wren was young,
So neatly as she danced,
And so sweetly as she sung—
Robin Redbreast lost his heart;
He was a gallant bird;
He doffed his hat to Jenny,
And thus to her he said:
"My dearest Jenny Wren,
If you will but be mine,
You shall dine on cherry pie,
And drink nice currant wine."
"I'll dress you like a goldfinch,
Or like a peacock gay;
So if you'll have me, Jenny,
Let us appoint the day."
While on his journey Puss, Jr., paused to listen to this

sweet song. On a branch above him sat Robin Redbreast. With his hat held in one claw he bowed most beautifully to a little wren that sat on a limb just below him. "I'll dress you like a goldfinch," repeated Robin, swinging his beautiful green hat with its long black feather up and down in the breeze.

Jenny blushed behind her fan,

And thus declared her mind:

"Then let it be to-morrow, Bob;

I'll take your offer kind.

"Cherry pie is very good,

So is currant wine;

But I'll wear my russet gown,

And never dress too fine."

"I'd like to buy her a beautiful gold dress," said Robin Redbreast, turning to look at Puss, Jr., who stood very quietly at the foot of the tree.

"I think her little russet gown is much nicer," replied Puss. "To tell you the truth, she wouldn't look very much like a wren if you dressed her like a goldfinch."

"Of course I wouldn't," chirruped little Jenny Wren; "and, besides, I wouldn't feel at all like myself. I might think Robin had married a goldfinch instead of me; and I don't want to think that."

"Of course you don't," said Puss, kindly.

"You are both right," said Robin Redbreast. "I only thought for the moment that she would like a different gown, but she shall have her way. There is only one little bird in the world for me, and that is Jenny Wren."

Jenny hid her face behind her fan, for she was I blushing very hard. Indeed, her cheeks were I almost as red as Robin's breast.

"To-morrow, then, shall be our wedding-day," said Robin, "and you are invited, my dear Puss, Junior."

PUSS AND SEVERAL ACQUAINTANCES JOURNEY TO THE WEDDING

ROBIN rose up early,
Before the break of day;
He flew to Jenny Wren's house,
To sing a roundelay.
He met the Cock and Hen,
And bade the Cock declare,
This should be his wedding-day,
With Jenny Wren, the fair.
The Cock then blew his horn,
To let the neighbors know
This was Robin's wedding-day,
And they might see the show.

Puss, Jr., was also up bright and early. He carefully polished his red-top boots and dusted his cap with the long feather in it. Then he started out for the woods.

"Cock-a-doodle-do!" cried the rooster.

"How do you doodle-do, my noble Sir Chanticleer?"

asked Puss, bowing. "I am on my way to Cock Robin's wedding; he has given me an invitation," he added, as the rooster stopped crowing to listen.

A little squirrel ran down from his tree and stood upright on his hind legs as Puss came to the edge of the woods. "Follow me," said Puss. "There is to be a fine wedding in your forest city this morning." So the little squirrel ran after Puss.

Presently they came to a little pond. On a big log sat a very friendly-looking old bullfrog. "Ker-chunk, ker-chunk!" he cried.

"Get off your log and come with us," said Puss, Jr. "There is to be a grand wedding in the woods."

The bullfrog jumped off his log into the water with a great splash and swam to the shore. Scrambling up the bank, he followed Puss and the squirrel. The three had only gone a little ways when they came to a chipmunk.

"Hello, Chip!" cried the little squirrel. "Don't you want to join us?"

"Where are you going?"

"To a wedding," said Puss, Jr.

"All right," said the chipmunk, and he ran up and joined Puss, Jr.'s, little party. After going for some distance they came to a brook.

"How shall we get across?" asked Puss, Jr.

"I'm all right," said the bullfrog. "I'll swim." And with a beautiful dive he landed in the middle of the stream and swam away to the other bank.

"I wish my boots were rubber," said Puss. "I might wade across and carry you two on my back."

While they were wondering what to do, a muskrat swam up to the bank and said: "Why don't you walk over Beaver Dam? It's only a little distance from here."

"Will it be perfectly safe?" asked the little squirrel, tim-idly.

"Certainly, my dear friends," replied the muskrat. "You run along the bank and I'll show you the way."

So Puss and his small comrades followed the little musk-rat till they reached Beaver Dam.

THE GUESTS ARRIVE SAFELY AT THE WEDDING

PUSS, JR., continued on his way with his small comrades, the squirrel, the old bullfrog, the chipmunk, the muskrat, the beaver (who had joined them without being asked after they had paid him for crossing his dam), and the timid little rabbit. Presently they saw in the distance the wedding procession of Cock Robin and Jenny Wren.

And first came Parson Rook,

With his spectacles and band,

And one of Mother Hubbard's books

He held within his hand.

The Sparrow and the Tomtit,

And many more, were there.

All came to see the wedding

Of Jenny Wren, the fair.

Then followed him the Lark,

For he could sweetly sing,

And he was to be the clerk

At Cock Robin's wedding.

"Let us make haste," cried Puss, Jr., "or we shall be late."

"Please don't go so fast," begged the old bullfrog. "I'm a very poor walker."

"Here, climb up on my back," said the squirrel. "You can lean against my tail. It will keep you from falling off."

This helped matters a great deal, and our little friends moved forward at a good pace. The old bullfrog was also much relieved. He was pretty tired and every once in a while gasped for breath. He was not too weary, however, to catch several flies on the way, and he winked quite solemnly at Puss, who grinned in return. As they neared the wedding procession they heard the lark singing.

He sang of Robin's love

For little Jenny Wren;

And when he came unto the end,

Then he began again.

The Goldfinch came on next,

To give away the bride;

The Linnet, being bridesmaid,

Walked by Jenny's side;

And as she was a-walking,

Said, "Upon my word,

I think that your Cock Robin

Is a very pretty bird."

"I think he is," whispered Puss, Jr., to the squirrel.

"So do I," said the chipmunk.

"Ker-chunk," said the old bullfrog, "he has a fine red vest. I always like white waistcoats, though," he added, looking down at his own; "but then, you know, everybody doesn't like the same thing."

PUSS IS WELCOMED AT THE WEDDING

ALL the birds of the forest seemed to be at the wedding of Cock Robin and little Jenny Wren, as Puss, Jr., and his little friends sat down beneath a big tree. The little squirrel cuddled up to Puss, while the chipmunk sat close by. The muskrat and the beaver stood near at hand, while the rabbit and the old bullfrog, who had climbed off the squirrel's back, looked out from behind the tree trunk. They were the most timid of all, so they hid behind the tree.

All the birds were singing as sweetly as could be. It was certainly very beautiful wedding music. Perhaps the most exquisite strains came from

The Blackbird and the Thrush,

And charming Nightingale,

Whose soft note sweetly echoes

Through every grove and dale;

The Bullfinch walked by Robin,

And thus to him did say:

"Pray mark, friend Robin Redbreast,

That Goldfinch dressed so gay;

"What though her gay apparel

Becomes her very well,

Yet Jenny's modest dress and look

Must bear away the bell."

Just then Parson Rook looked over at them. "Why, Puss in Boots, Junior!" he called out. "Come over here," and, turning to the wedding guests, he said: "There is the son of the famous Puss in Boots. We are honored to have so illustrious a person with us. And delighted, too, for he is a great traveler and a jolly good fellow."

Puss, Jr., arose and bowed.

"Bring your little friends with you, also," said Parson Rook, "for all the forest folk are welcome. Who is there more loved, I would like to know, than Robin Redbreast and little Jenny Wren?"

"Nobody!" croaked the old bullfrog.

"No one," said Puss, Jr.

"We all love Robin and Jenny," cried the squirrel and the chipmunk.

"And so do I," "And so do I," cried the beaver and the rabbit together. As they finished the birds began to sing the wedding-march.

Then came the bride and bridegroom,

Quite plainly was she dressed,

And blushed so much, her cheeks were

As red as Robin's breast.

But Robin cheered her up;

"My pretty Jen," said he,

"We're going to be married,

And happy we shall be."

"I'm going to give her a gold piece for good luck," whispered Puss.

"I've got a nut," said the little squirrel.

"And so have I!" said the chipmunk. "We'll each give her a nut."

"I'll give her a fresh-water pearl," said the old bullfrog.

The rabbit and the beaver looked at each other. "We'll have to run home and get something," they cried.

THE BRIDE RECEIVES SOME HANDSOME PRESENTS

"DON'T be gone long," cried Puss, Jr., as the rabbit and the beaver ran off to their homes to get a present for Jenny Wren. "You had better hurry, or the wedding will be over by the time you return."

"Don't worry about me," said the rabbit, whisking away at a great rate.

"I'll be back, never fear," said the beaver.

Puss watched them out of sight, then he heard the parson begin again:

"Oh, then," says Parson Rook,

"Who gives this maid away?"

"I do," says the Goldfinch,

"And her fortune I will pay;

"Here's a bag of grain of many sorts,

And other things besides;

Now happy be the bridegroom,

And happy be the bride."

Presently the rabbit returned. "Do you think she will like this?" he asked Puss, Jr., holding up a little white powder-puff. "I made it all myself. I had it put away in a little box for safe-keeping."

"It's very pretty," said Puss, Jr., with a smile. "What little bunny's tail did you cut off to make it with?"

"Not mine," replied the rabbit; "but don't ask me too many questions."

Just then the beaver came panting up. "Whew!" he cried. "I'd rather travel by water than by land; but, anyhow, I'm here. How do you think she will like my present?" and he held up a little gold ring.

"Just the thing!" cried Puss. "But where did you get it?"

"Oh, I found it on the bottom of the brook one day," replied the beaver, "so I picked it up and hung it on a nail; I thought it might come in handy some day."

"When shall we give her the present?" asked the squirrel.

"Wait, wait," said Puss; "they are not yet married. Listen to Parson Rook:

"And will you have her, Robin,

To be your wedded wife?"

"Yes, I will," says Robin,

"And love her all my life."

"And will you have him, Jenny,

Your husband now to be?"

"Yes, I will," says Jenny,

"And love him heartily!"

Then on her finger fair

Cock Robin put the ring;

"You're married now," says Parson Rook,

While loud the lark did sing:

"Happy be the bridegroom,

And happy be the bride,

And may not man, nor bird, nor beast,

This happy pair divide."

PUSS MAKES A NEW FRIEND AND GAINS A STEED

"HEIGH-HO!" cried Puss, Jr., swinging his cane, as he marched merrily along—"heigh-ho for a short journey and a happy ending!"

"Well said, my merric Lord Cat," cried a voice. A tinker by the roadside looked up as Puss was about to pass him by.

"If wishes were horses, beggars would ride.

If turnips were watches,

I'd wear one at my side.

And if 'ifs' and 'ands'

Were pots and pans,

There'd be no work for tinkers!"

"I guess you are right, my good sir," said Puss, pausing and looking at the old tins that the tinker had set down on the ground. "If wishes were horses, I'd have one at once, for four legs are better than two, and horses' legs are meant to travel, while a cat's are not made especially for that purpose."

"You are an observing cat," said the tinker, with a twinkle in his eye.

"I speak from experience, my good man," said Puss, "for I have used my legs for traveling these many miles, and when I look at a horse, I cannot help thinking he has the better of me as far as legs go."

"And when I look at my legs," said the tinker, "I think how well they would look astride of a good gray horse."

"Let us both make a wish," suggested Puss, half in fun and half in earnest. "Wishes do come true at times, you know."

"I GUESS YOU ARE RIGHT, MY GOOD SIR," SAID PUSS

"Very good," replied the tinker, "I'm wishing."

"And so am I," said Puss.

To their utter astonishment they heard a shrill neigh close at hand, and, turning to see what manner of steed had answered so quickly their wishes, they beheld two fine gray horses in the meadow close by. Leaning their heads over the fence rail, the two animals gazed at them with expectant eyes.

"Why, they already have on their saddles and bridles!" cried the tinker, with amazement. "Are you a fairy cat? Do your wishes always come true?"

"That is a nice question to answer," replied Puss, "but in this case, you can see for yourself."

"Well," said the tinker, "let us not refuse this stroke of good luck. I, for one, shall mount one of yonder steeds."

"I GUESS YOU ARE RIGHT, MY GOOD SIR," SAID PUSS

"And I will ride the other," cried Puss, nimbly springing over the fence. Thrusting his foot into the stirrup, he sprang into the saddle and waited for his friend the tinker. Alas for the clumsy tinker! As he attempted to mount, the bundle of old tins made such a rattle that both horses jumped in fright, and in another moment ran off at a great rate. Puss clung tightly to the reins, and, on looking back, saw the bewildered tinker still standing by the fence, while his horse careered across the meadow, kicking up his heels and snorting at a great rate.

PUSS MEETS A HUNTER AND THEY BOTH LEARN THAT THE OWL IS A USEFUL BIRD

WELL, that was a clumsy tinker," said Puss to himself, as he guided his good gray horse into the highway. "But I suppose he is no rider, and therefore is safer upon his own two legs. At any rate, I cannot stop to inquire, nor would I be of any assistance. So I shall ride away, thankful at my good luck in having a steed for a mere wish. As wishes are horses, pussy-cats may ride," he said, with a laugh.

The gray horse proved a good roadster and covered many a mile before midday. Presently, on coming to a crossway, Puss decided to take the road that led through the woods. He had hardly entered when he saw a funny little man dressed like a huntsman. In his right hand he carried a bow and on his back was a quiver full of arrows.

A small dog ran along at his heels, snuffing about continually, as if expecting to find a rabbit or a squirrel. Before Puss had gone much farther, the funny little huntsman paused under a large tree, from a hole in which an old owl looked out, winking and blinking his eyes.

There was an owl lived in an oak,
Whiskey, Whaskey, Weedle;
And all the words he ever spoke
Were Fiddle, Faddle, Feedle.
A sportsman chanced to come that way,
Whiskey, Whaskey, Weedle;
Said he, "I'll shoot you, silly bird!"
So Fiddle, Faddle, Feedle.

"Bow-wow!" yelped the little dog, suddenly catching sight of the old owl.

"There now, you've gone and done it!" cried the funny little hunter, as the owl quickly drew in his head. "You're a fine hunting-dog, you are!"

The little dog hung his tail and walked away. In another moment, on catching sight of Puss on his big gray horse, he set up another wild barking.

"What's the matter now?" inquired the little huntsman. "Oh, it's you, is it?" he exclaimed, suddenly seeing Puss.

"Your little dog is a better watchman than a hunter," said Puss, with a grin; "that is, he's a good old scout."

"Well, I'm glad to find out he's good for something," said the little hunter, "for he made me just now lose a good shot at an old owl that has been hooting and tooting around my house for many nights. I would have liked to put an arrow through his old head."

"You would, eh?" screamed the owl, suddenly poking his head through the hole. "Let me tell you, my good sir, that I have caught more rats and mice in your old barn than your cat has. Is this the way that you repay a useful friend like me?"

The little hunter dropped his bow. "I never thought of that," he said, apologetically.

"Well, next time think before you shoot," cried the owl; "it may save you many a miss!"

PUSS GOES ON A SHOPPING TRIP TO MAKE A LITTLE MAID HAPPY

THE rose is red, the violet blue;

    The gillyflower's sweet, and so are you.

These are the words you bade me say

For a pair of new gloves on Easter Day."

Puss, Jr., looked down from his horse at a little girl who was swinging on the front gate. He pulled up his good gray horse:

"A pair of new gloves on Easter Day? Is that what you want the most?"

"Yes, indeed," cried the little girl. "I've got a new bonnet with red ribbons on it, and also a gown of yellow and brown; a pair of silk hose of the color of rose, and a lovely new pin with a big diamond in. A parasol, too, of purple and blue."

"Wait a minute," said Puss, "you talk so fast, and your words all rhyme, and you've got so many things, of so many different colors that—that I really don't remember whether you said you had a pair of gloves, after all."

"No, my dear pussy-cat," said the little maid, with a

pout. "I have new shoes, and new everything but gloves. Now won't you bring me a pair for Easter Day?"

"Where shall I buy them?" asked Puss. "I don't see any shops about, and if I must go all the way to London for them you'll never receive them in time for this Easter."

"Not far from here," cried the little maid, "is a tiny shop where they make beautiful gloves. Take the first road to your right and then turn to your left, and then turn to your right, and then you'll see it."

"Whew! Mew!" cried Puss. "Well, here goes. I'll do the best I can, but if I do not return you will know that I turned to the left when I should have turned to the right, and then that I turned to the right when I should have turned to the left, and so got all mixed up and never found the tiny shop where the beautiful gloves are made." This was a long sentence for Puss, but he was learning how to make conversation after the manner of little girls!

But his good gray horse must have remembered the directions, for he landed his small master safe at the glove-shop. Puss, Jr., bought a lovely pair of gloves and remounted his horse. Soon he was back again in front of the little gate where a short half-hour before the little girl had been swinging back and forth. She had disappeared, but he heard her singing.

"Where are the gloves for Easter Day?" she cried, running out of the door of the cottage.

"Here they are, my pretty one," said Puss.

"The rose is red, the violet blue;

The gillyflower's sweet, and so are you,"

sang the little girl as she tried them on.

"These are the words you bade me say

For a pair of new gloves on Easter Day,

"Aren't they, dear Puss, Junior?" she said, with a smile, looking up at him.

PUSS CONVERSES WITH AN INTELLIGENT GRAY DONKEY

D ONKEY, donkey, old and gray,
　　Ope your mouth and gently bray,
Lift your ears and blow your horn
To wake the world this sleepy morn,"
called Puss, Jr., who always remembered his Mother Goose rhymes perfectly.

The donkey paused in his grazing and looked up. "This sleepy morn," he repeated. "I don't call this a 'sleepy morn.' I should say it was very wide awake."

"I guess it is," admitted Puss, "but, you see, I was only saying a little rhyme from Mother Goose."

"Well, I don't see how it applies to the present situation at all," replied the donkey, in a rather ungracious manner. "The only thing you have right is the donkey part."

Puss felt rather crestfallen. To be corrected by a donkey, generally considered one of the stupidest of animals, was not at all to his liking. Puss evidently forgot for the moment that all Mother Goose animals are very intelligent, for otherwise how would they have been celebrated in rhyme? But, like a wise cat, he took the rebuke meekly and said nothing.

"Well," said the donkey, after a pause, "can I do anything else for you, Sir Cat? Granting that it is too late to wake the morn, there may be other requests with which I will gladly comply."

"Gracious me!" thought Puss to himself, "he uses big words."

The donkey cocked up both ears as if awaiting Puss, Jr.'s, reply.

"Which is the shorter road across Mother Goose Land?" inquired Puss.

"I don't know the exact number of miles," replied the donkey, thoughtfully, "but the road to your left is the shorter. The one to your right leads to the seashore. Gingerbread Bridge is at the ending."

"What!" exclaimed Puss, Jr. "Why, you don't say so!"

"What do you know about Gingerbread Bridge?" asked the donkey.

"I crossed it once, and not so very long ago, either," replied Puss.

"Then you certainly don't want to take Gingerbread Road," replied the donkey, "so it is not hard to choose which way to go."

"Thank you," said Puss, turning his horse's head down the road to the left. "I will take the left road because it is the right road!"

"Ha, ha!" brayed the donkey, "that's a good joke for a cat. May you have a pleasant journey!"

"Lift your ears and blow your horn; the sheep's in the meadow, the cows' in the corn!" cried Puss, gaily. "Although the morn is awake, I fear Boy Blue is still asleep."

And with these words our small hero cantered down the road and out of sight.

PUSS MEETS A HAPPY FARMER BUT MISSES A GOOD MEAL

TOWARD noon of a fine day Puss, Jr., halted his good gray horse near a meadow. Standing near the fence, sharpening his scythe, stood a young farmer. His wide straw hat kept off the sun and his loose shirt and open collar let in the breeze which was blowing across the green grass.

"Warm day," said Puss, as he drew rein.

"Well," replied the farmer, "it's not so bad. I don't feel it." And he commenced to sing:

"My maid Mary she minds the dairy,

While I go a-hoeing and mowing each morn,

Gaily run the reel and the little spinning-wheel,

Whilst I am singing and mowing my corn."

"Are farmers always so happy?" asked Puss when the man stopped singing.

The farmer smiled and said: "My good sir, when one is blessed with a fine wife and a good farm he can beat a canary-bird at singing."

"You don't say so!" said Puss, Jr. "But suppose one has neither, what should such an unlucky one do?"

"Don't ask me," said the farmer, setting to work again. "I'm a simple man, and what is happiness for me might not be for another."

As he swung his scythe back and forth the tall grass fell in graceful rows and the sweet scent of the new-mown hay was everywhere. Suddenly Puss saw a field-mouse scampering over the ground. This was too much for Puss. He had eaten nothing since breakfast, and he had not had a mouse to eat for so long that he had almost forgotten how mice tasted. Jumping down from his good gray horse, he gave chase.

"Go it, Sir Cat!" cried the farmer. "Don't lose him."

Puss needed no words of encouragement. He longed for a good run, and his mouth fairly watered at the idea of a nice fat little mouse for lunch. But the field-mouse saw him coming and wasted no time. Away he went, hopping over the grass and looking wildly about for a place in which to hide. A trunk of a fallen tree at no great distance attracted his attention, and with a final burst of speed he reached it and crawled into a hole before Puss had the opportunity to seize him by the tail.

"Oh, pshaw!" cried Puss, sitting down on the log. "I surely thought I had him."

"You did, eh?" squeaked the little mouse, peering out of his hole and laughing at poor Puss. "I prefer to be inside this log rather than inside even so famous a character as Puss in Boots, Junior."

"How do you know my name?" asked Puss, surprised at what he heard.

"Why, I'm one of the three blind mice whose tails the farmer's wife cut off," said the mouse.

"I thought there was very little tail to you," said Puss, "or else you went into the hole so fast that it made your tail look very short, for I couldn't even get a little hold on it."

"Well, having my tail clipped did me some good," said the mouse.

PUSS HELPS A STRANGER CATCH A RUNAWAY PIG

To market, to market, to buy a fat pig,
    Home again, home again, jiggety jig.
To market, to market, to buy a fat hog,
Home again, home again, jiggety jog.
To market, to market, to buy a plum bun,
Home again, home again, market is done."

A funny little man came dancing down the road. Before him he drove a fat pig, which squeaked and grunted loudly. To one of its hind legs was fastened a rope, the other end of which the funny little man held tightly in his hand.

"To market, to market, to buy a fat pig,

Home again, home again, jiggety jig."

sang the little old man. "How do you like my piggety pig?" he asked, looking up at Puss, Jr., who had stopped his good gray horse to watch the funny sight.

"He looks like a fine pig," replied Puss.

"Whoa, there, piggety pig!" cried the old man as the pig

"TO MARKET, TO MARKET, TO BUY A FAT PIG"

began to struggle to get away.

"Look out!" cried Puss. But the warning came too late. The pig had wriggled his foot out of the noose and went racing down the road.

"Take me up behind you!" cried the little old man. "Then let us follow and catch him."

"Jump up! Quick about it!" cried Puss, Jr.

In a moment the little old man was on the good gray horse, who immediately set off at a gallop to overtake the piggety pig. It was a long race, for he had a good head start and terror lent wings to his feet.

"Git up!" cried Puss, digging his heels into the sides of the good gray horse. "Git up! Don't you see the pig is getting away from us?"

"Neigh, neigh!" cried the good gray horse as he gave a spring forward.

"Then go faster!" screamed the little old man.

"Gid ap!" yelled Puss, Jr. At this the horse with leaps and bounds came closer and closer to the fleeing pig.

"I've got the rope!" cried the little old man.

"Make a big noose at one end," said Puss, "and as we draw near throw it over his head."

"That I will," answered the little old man. "When I was young I was a cowboy. I hope I've not forgotten how to swing a lariat."

As good luck would have it, he had not. All at once the little old man swung the rope in the air and the noose fell over the pig's head.

"I've got him! I've got him!" cried the old man, and Puss, Jr., pulled in his horse. The race was over and the old man, jumping down to the ground, thanked Puss again and again for his assistance.

PUSS HELPS A LITTLE BOY WHO IS IN TROUBLE

THE town of Banbury Cross was very pretty, situated at the corner of two cross-roads, close to a sparkling river over which ran a bridge. As Puss, Jr., on his good gray horse, whose feet went rackety-rackety, rackety-tak over the broad planking, drew rein at the farther end a small boy, who stood by the side of a pretty little pony, began to sing:

"I had a little pony,

His name was Dapple-gray,

I lent him to a lady

To ride a mile away.

She whipped him, she lashed him,

She rode him through the mire;

I would not lend my pony now,

For all the lady's hire."

"Neither would I," said Puss.

The little boy opened his eyes very wide. They were blue as the skies overhead and were full of tears. "She whipped him, she lashed him," continued the boy. "I'll never again lend my pony to anybody."

"I wouldn't lend my good gray horse," said Puss, "for one never knows whether a person is kind to animals or not."

"I never thought a lady would hurt my pony," sobbed the boy. "Just look at him. He's all covered with mud."

"So he is," said Puss, consolingly; "but never mind. A good washing will fix him up."

"But my father will be angry," said the boy. "He doesn't like to wash my pony, and I'm too little."

"Let's take your pony down to the riverbank," Puss suggested. "We'll find a shallow spot and wash him off. Perhaps we can ride him a little way into the water; that would help." Tying his good gray horse to a post near by, Puss led the pony down the bank to the river, the little boy following.

"Do you want to ride him in," asked Puss, "or shall I?"

"You do it," said the little boy. "I'm afraid."

So Puss jumped on the pony's back and gently urged him into the river. After going out some distance he stopped, for the water was almost up to his boots. "I guess I can wash him now," cried Puss, and, leaning over, first on one side and then on the other, he splashed up the water and scrubbed off the mud and dirt until the pony was as clean as a whistle.

"Now," exclaimed Puss, "he looks like himself again." The pony seemed quite relieved also, for after gaining the bank he neighed and kicked up his heels in a delighted manner.

"He looks better than ever," said the little boy. "He was really quite dusty before I lent him to the lady."

"Yes, he's in fine shape," said Puss. "I must now leave you, for I am on a long journey."

"Thank you," said the boy. "A pleasant journey to you, my good Sir Cat."

How our little hero, Puss in Boots, Jr., at last finds his famous father, Puss in Boots, at the castle of my Lord of Carabas, will be told in Further Adventures of Puss in Boots, Jr.

THE END

9 789355 178251